MY CARIBBEAN GRANDMA

SANDRA CAMPBELL - NOTICE

Illustrations by Anura Srinath

Edited by Natasha S. Notice

Brer Anancy Press

First Edition
ISBN: 978-9768266019

Ordering Information:
Quantity sales. Special discounts are available on quantity purchases by corporations, associations, and others. For details contact

Brer Anancy Press
P.O. Box 361582
Los Angeles, CA 90036
info@breranancypress.com   bluemountainrhythms@gmail.com
www.breranancypress.com   www.bluemountainrhythms.com

Printed in the United States of America

Dedication

This book is dedicated to the memory of

my maternal grandmother

Timinisha A. Stewart-Thomas.

It is also dedicated to

my daughters Tinisha and Natasha

who encourage me daily

to do all the things

I want to do.

THEY ARE MY TRUE LOVE

AND MY INSPIRATION.

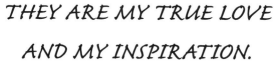

MY CARIBBEAN GRANDMA

Ms. Timinisha Stewart-Thomas was my Caribbean grandma. She was a shy, loving, patient, and dedicated woman who always wore a smile on her face.

When I think of my Caribbean grandma, I'm reminded of her long, thick, black hair, her short plump body, and her round face. Her skin was the perfect blend of the brown rich soil, and her loving eyes seemed to twinkle just like the rays of sunshine glistening on the waters of the Caribbean Sea.

6

Grandma was an extremely hardworking woman.
As soon as the sun rose over the Blue Mountains,
she cooked a healthy breakfast over the open fire
for the family. Often we would have green bananas,
callaloo and saltfish, and a cup of peppermint tea.
After breakfast, she would gather buckets of water,
clean the house and yard, then go to her gardens
and tend to the crops.

Most of grandma's day would be spent inspecting or picking fruits, pulling weeds from the vegetable gardens, tilling the soil, transplanting crops, or making sure the soil received enough fertilizer to make the vegetables she planted grow healthy. While grandma did her chores, my brother, sister, and I would make sure that all of the plants got enough water to keep them healthy and growing.

When the fruits and vegetables were ready, grandma would spend hours harvesting them. My brother and sister would help her to pull the carrots, turnips, and beets from the ground, while grandma would take care of the scallions, rosemary, tomatoes, scotch bonnet peppers, and other crops. I would sometimes glance at my grandmother and smile to myself, as I watch her work and listen to her tell my brother and sister what to do. My favorite thing to do was to pull the thyme from the ground and put the bundles in the basket nearby.

After we took the crops home,
my brother, sister and I would
help grandma wash the vegetables
in a large tub of water we had gathered,
tie them and the seasonings into small
bundles, then pack them into baskets
and burlap squares, ready for sale
at the market.

The look on grandma's face as we sorted and packed the crops was one filled with delight. The crops she had planted, cared for, and harvested were now ready for others to enjoy. She was now more than anxious to go to the market in the city to sell her crops.

Early on a Thursday morning, grandma
would get ready for her trip to the market.
She would cook our breakfast then iron
her favorite plaid dress. The dress was the
folk attire for most of the women
who lived on the island, and was worn
whenever they went to the market.
Along with the dress, Grandma would
put on her brown stockings and lace up
her shiny black shoes on her feet.
She would then tie her head with a scarf
that matched her dress, and a plait of
her thick black hair would be left out just
above her forehead.

While grandma dressed, my brother, sister, and I placed all the bags and baskets by the front gate, and waited for the arrival of the jeep that would take Grandma to her destination. Grandma smiled at us when she came to the gate, and told my brother to be good while she was away.

When the Land-Rover jeep arrived, the driver's helper loaded grandma's goods onto the top of the vehicle, while grandma climbed into the back and sat with the other ladies. Her trip to the market had begun and she would travel with the other women for hours over unpaved roads to the market in the city.

The city market was one of the busiest, and most colorful places in the city. It was like a beautiful mural. The large open-air structure, built of concrete and wood, was always filled with people buying and selling a variety of items. The colors of the fruits, vegetables, clothes, and household items were everywhere!

Not only was the market colorful,
but it was also a very noisy place with
people talking, laughing, bargaining,
and arguing. Sometimes people would
be very playful, teasing each other,
and running throughout the stalls.
Although my grandma was a bit timid,
she always fit in with the crowd.

At grandma's wooden stall, she greeted her customers with a cheerful smile as they said hello to her. Each customer would purchase some of the thyme, rosemary, scallions, carrots, turnips, beets, scotch bonnet peppers, tomatoes, cho-cho, and other fruits and vegetables grandma had brought to the market. Some customers would bargain with grandma for a lower price and if she were in the mood, she would sell the item for that price and say, "You got a bargain!"

25

Saturday evening is when grandma would return home from the market. When my brother, sister, and I heard the horn of the jeep blowing, we would run to the front gate to greet grandma as the jeep stopped to drop her off. As grandma waved good-bye to the other women, we would quickly grab the bags filled with food items needed for the family. There would be sweetened milk, flour, cornmeal, rice, meat, fish, bread, butter, and cooking oil. We also searched for candy and any other surprise treats she may have brought home for us. This time, grandma brought pieces of candy, coconut cakes, and fried sprats. We ate our tasty treats in seconds and grandma smiled.

As we sat comfortably around grandma's feet, our faces lit up listening to the stories about her trip to the market. She told us about the journey going and coming on the packed jeep where there was usually not much room to breathe! She told us about the people she saw at the market, what she sold, what she ate, and who talked with her while she sold her crops. We always wanted to know if our older cousin who now lived in the city, had visited her. If she said he did, we would smile broadly.

Grandma also told us that because of the heavy rain in the lower part of the community, it was dangerous for the jeep to drive through the Yallahs River. It was deep, wide, and high, so she and the other women had to walk across the bridge and transfer all of their supplies to the big Leyland truck that was waiting on the other side of the river.

Many of the ladies she said, were scared to walk across the bridge because it was old and squeaky, and the big, muddy river was directly below. What if the bridge collapsed and someone fell in?

That thought alone made them not want to walk across the bridge but the men who were there helped them to walk safely over. Grandma said she was scared but tried not to think about the danger. She held on tightly to one of the men and told him if she fell in, he would be going too. That made everyone close to her laugh out loud. We were always excited to hear stories about grandma's adventurous journey to the market.

That night as we went to sleep,
I thought about the garden,
the jeep, the market, the river, the
truck, the stories, and my wonderful
grandma who slept quietly beside
me. I saw many pictures in my
head and wondered when
I would be able to go to the
market with grandma to see
all the things she had seen.

Weeks would pass and as soon as grandma had planted, cared for, and harvested more seasonings, fruits and vegetables, it was time once again to make another trip to the market. This was a never-ending cycle for her and the other women who lived in the rural areas of the island.

On this trip, my sister and I would go with grandma to the market. We were excited! It was our turn to have an adventure with my Caribbean grandma.

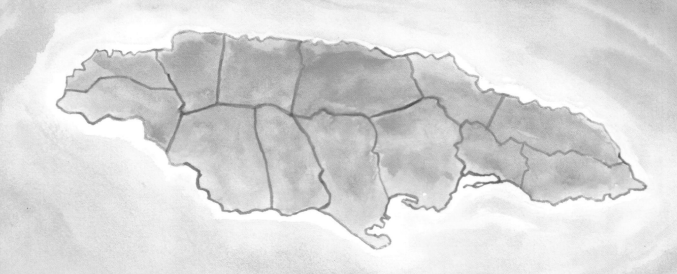

Map of Jamaica